The Emperor's New Clothes

Puss 'N Boots
Aladdin and the Magic Lamp
Copyright © 1969 by
Fratelli Fabbri Editori, Milan, Italy
Published by Fratelli Fabbri Editori Publishers,
Milan, Italy and
The McCall Publishing Company, New York, New York
Printed in Italy

Once upon a time there lived an emperor who was very vain indeed. He spent the whole day trying on new clothes and admiring himself in the mirror. In fact, he used most of his royal riches to buy exquisite clothing so he would be admired. The emperor passed so much time changing and trying on clothes that whenever someone wanted to see him, the palace guards would say, ''He is before the mirror. We cannot disturb him.'' Or else they would say, ''The emperor has gone to see an elegant costume.''

2

One fine day two dishonest rascals appeared in the emperor's city. They did not come to admire the city like most travelers. Instead, they came to rob the emperor of some of his riches. They knew of his weakness for fine clothing, and they had a plan: they would make the emperor a beautiful suit of clothes,

3

unlike any he had ever seen. And so
they began to set up their weaver's tools.

DOREMI — Is the loom ready for weaving?

FASOLA — Yes, we are ready to carry out our plan.

So, after setting up the loom, they wandered through the city,
spreading the news of the arrival of two famous weavers.
The news reached the town gossip, who began telling
everyone in sight...

4

GOSSIP — Have you heard? Two weavers have arrived in town. They are known to be the best in twenty kingdoms. I have been told they weave marvelous materials, that are not only beautiful but also magical. Imagine! The cloth can only be seen by those who are truly intelligent. Fools cannot see it, although they might pretend they can. But, to fools, it is absolutely invisible.

The moment the emperor found out about this magical material, he became very excited...

EMPEROR — I must have a suit made of this marvelous cloth. The wardrobe of an emperor cannot be missing such an outfit. Also... aha... since fools cannot see it, I shall learn which of my advisors are fools. Yes, it is absolutely necessary that I have such a magical suit. I shall summon these two famous weavers immediately.

A little later...

DOREMI — We are at your service, Your Majesty.

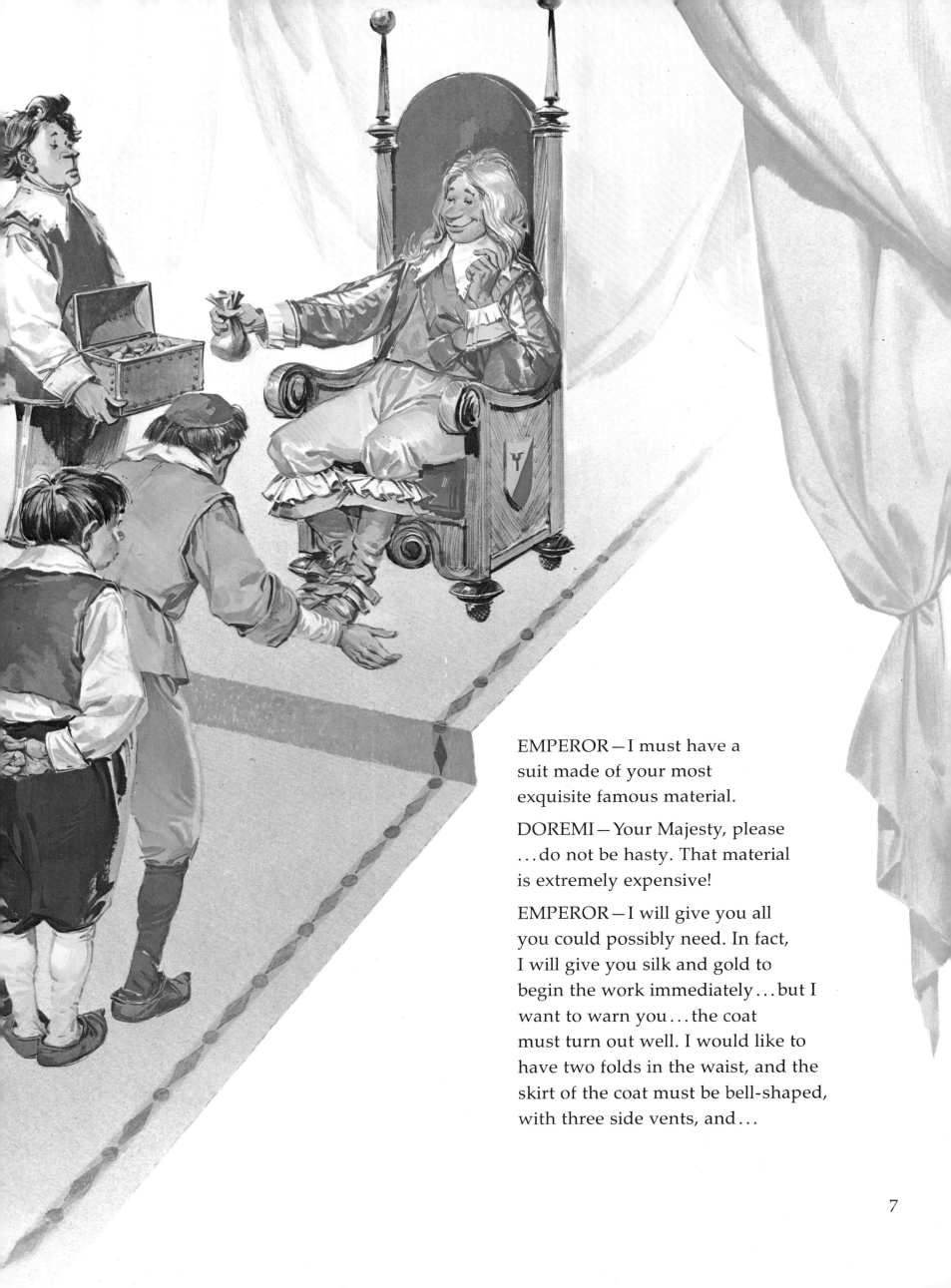

EMPEROR—I must have a
suit made of your most
exquisite famous material.

DOREMI—Your Majesty, please
…do not be hasty. That material
is extremely expensive!

EMPEROR—I will give you all
you could possibly need. In fact,
I will give you silk and gold to
begin the work immediately…but I
want to warn you…the coat
must turn out well. I would like to
have two folds in the waist, and the
skirt of the coat must be bell-shaped,
with three side vents, and…

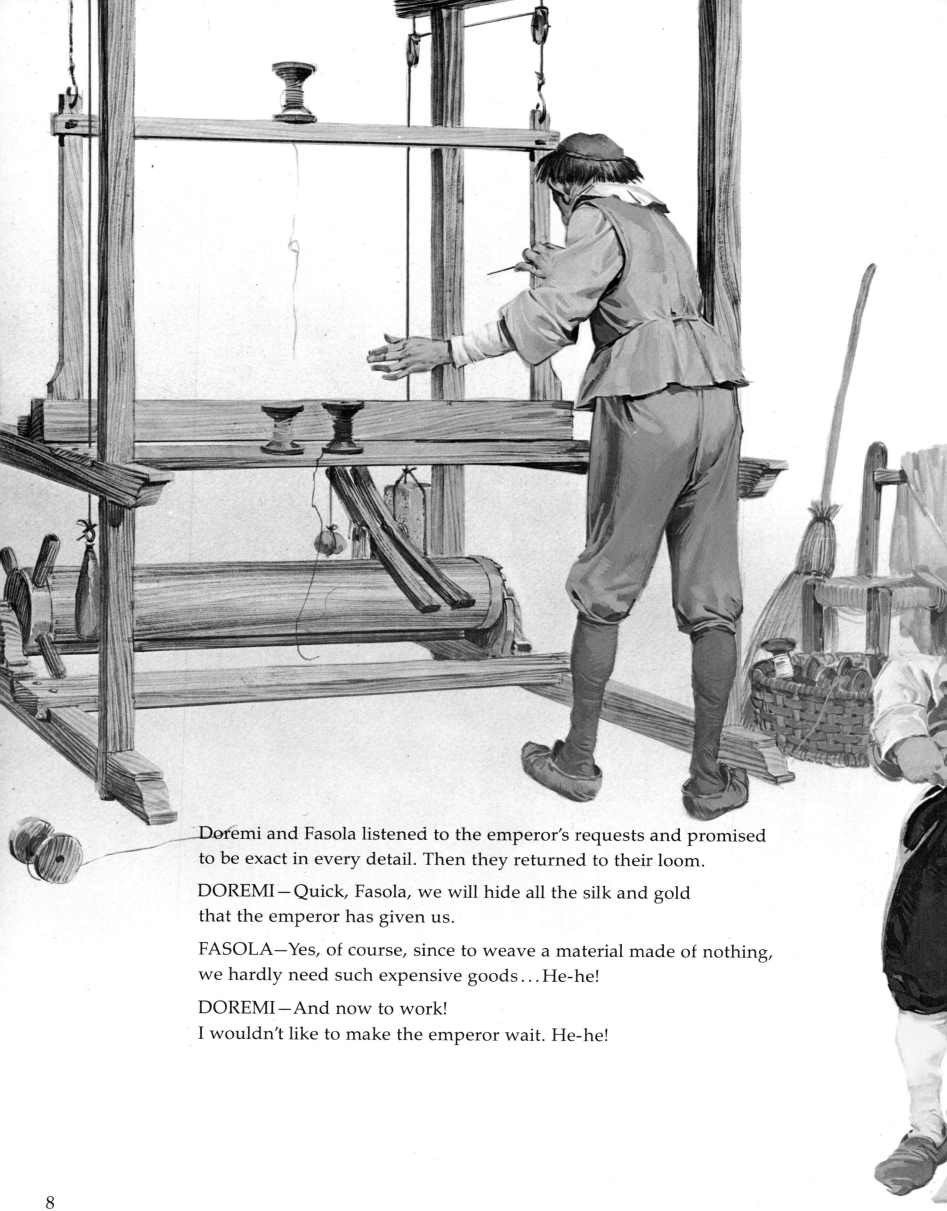

Doremi and Fasola listened to the emperor's requests and promised to be exact in every detail. Then they returned to their loom.

DOREMI—Quick, Fasola, we will hide all the silk and gold that the emperor has given us.

FASOLA—Yes, of course, since to weave a material made of nothing, we hardly need such expensive goods...He-he!

DOREMI—And now to work!
I wouldn't like to make the emperor wait. He-he!

8

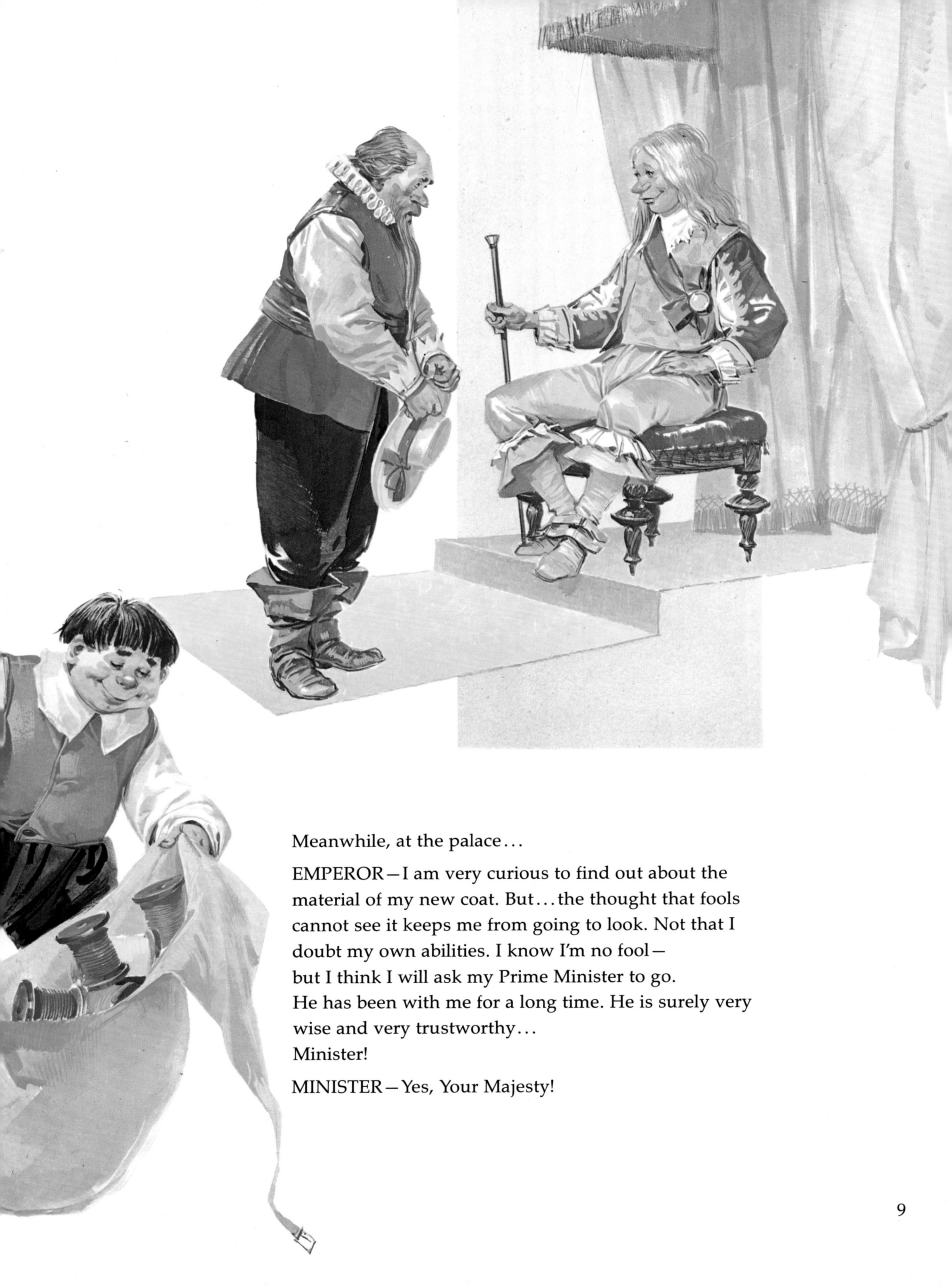

Meanwhile, at the palace...

EMPEROR—I am very curious to find out about the material of my new coat. But...the thought that fools cannot see it keeps me from going to look. Not that I doubt my own abilities. I know I'm no fool— but I think I will ask my Prime Minister to go. He has been with me for a long time. He is surely very wise and very trustworthy...
Minister!

MINISTER—Yes, Your Majesty!

EMPEROR—Go see the weavers
and find out how they're coming
along. Inspect the material
and tell me how you like it.
I depend upon your judgment.

MINISTER—As you desire, Sire!

The minister, of course, knew
the story of the magic material.
Therefore, he knocked at the
weavers' door somewhat timidly.
The weavers opened the door,
saw the minister, and
grinned at each other.

DOREMI—Come in, come in,
dear minister! Look how well
the job is going!
Fasola, stand back, and let the
minister have a good look…

MINISTER—Where should I look?

FASOLA—But here, of course,
on the loom!

MINISTER—(Oh, woe is me!
I don't see anything!…So I must
be a fool, incapable of
performing my duties.)

10

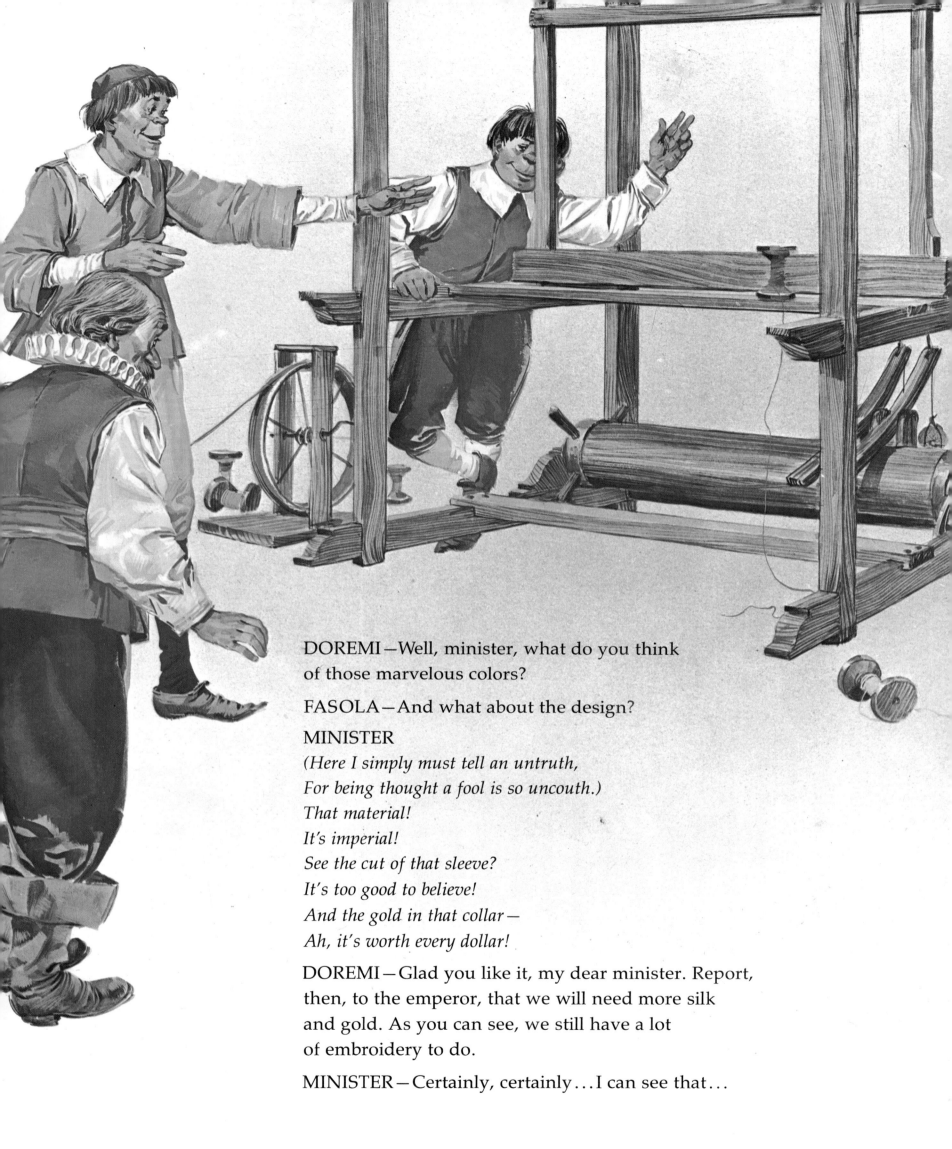

DOREMI—Well, minister, what do you think
of those marvelous colors?

FASOLA—And what about the design?

MINISTER
(*Here I simply must tell an untruth,*
For being thought a fool is so uncouth.)
That material!
It's imperial!
See the cut of that sleeve?
It's too good to believe!
And the gold in that collar—
Ah, it's worth every dollar!

DOREMI—Glad you like it, my dear minister. Report,
then, to the emperor, that we will need more silk
and gold. As you can see, we still have a lot
of embroidery to do.

MINISTER—Certainly, certainly…I can see that…

The minister returned to the emperor.

EMPEROR—Well, Minister, have you seen the material?

MINISTER—How can you doubt it?
Do you take me for a fool?

EMPEROR—Well, how *is* the material, then?

MINISTER—Beautiful, stupendous! The weave is so fine you almost cannot see it. All the gold is intertwined like this...and then like that. Oh, it's a marvel! Not to speak of the silk...that silk...

EMPEROR—Yes, I know. I gave them that silk. But I am glad the work goes well.

MINISTER—Yes, but the weavers need more gold and silk.

EMPEROR—What for?

MINISTER—You must understand...I have seen with my own eyes, they still have much embroidering left to do.

EMPEROR—I understand...
certainly...I shall send a
dignitary with more gold
and silk, and he can see
the material too.
Dignitary!

DIGNITARY—Yes, Your Highness!

EMPEROR—Take these to the weavers.

DIGNITARY—Why me, Your Highness?

The dignitary was afraid that he
would be unable to see the material,
because, in his heart, he believed

himself to be a fool. But he took the gold and silk and went to the weavers. He found them working hard, busily running imaginary threads throughout the entire room. The dignitary, who could see absolutely nothing, went forward into the room and...

DOREMI—Watch out! You're standing on the material!

DIGNITARY—(Goodness! The material *is* invisible! I must act as if I see it!) How beautiful! What gorgeous colors! Here is the gold and the silk that you need to finish the work.

FASOLA—Thank you. You can see how much we need these for the embroidery.

DIGNITARY—Oh, by all means! I shall tell the emperor that the work is going beautifully. Very stylish, indeed! My-my, yes.

And the dignitary returned to the emperor.

DIGNITARY—The weavers are doing an excellent job, Your Majesty. An excellent job. Yes, sir!

EMPEROR—Good! Tomorrow I'll go see this marvelous material myself.

Next day, the emperor, escorted by the minister and the dignitary,
went to see the weavers, who were busy at their loom.
When the emperor entered the room,
the minister and the dignitary, afraid to give the impression

that they did not see anything, tried to outdo each other
with praises of the invisible material.

MINISTER—Look at those colors, Your Highness.

DIGNITARY—Magnificent material! Is it not, Sire?

MINISTER—And the embroidery? Enchanting!

The two poor fools competed with each other, pointing at the
loom where the invisible material was being woven.

DIGNITARY—And that red—stupendous! And what a yellow!

DOREMI—But don't you see, my dear sir, that it is green
and blue? Do you see it or not?

DIGNITARY—Yes, you are right. How stupid of me!

The emperor, meanwhile, was attempting to see the material.
But as hard as he tried, he could see nothing.

EMPEROR—(This is terrible! I must be the only fool! I just cannot see that material! Poor me! No one will know, of course. I shall simply *pretend* to see it!) Magnificent! Absolutely beautiful. Oh, how satisfied I am! Beautiful, really beautiful! Those colors! My good fellows, good-by. For the fitting of the coat, I suggest, be on time. Oh, I *am* delighted!

And the emperor returned to his coach, while the two weavers held their sides with laughter.

WEAVERS

The emperor's men were fighting a duel —
Over which of them was the greatest fool!
But our emperor entered and won the brawl,
And came out as the biggest fool of all!
This whole fiasco certainly shows
That foolish is he who lives only for clothes.
And, oh how his subjects will snicker and stare
When the emperor appears in his <u>underwear!</u>

There were only two days left until the grand
feast. It was for this feast that the
emperor was to lead a procession about the city.
He would be in full view of all his subjects,
and he wanted to look his very best.
So he planned to wear his new suit of clothes.
The two cunning weavers said they no longer
slept, but worked all night, in order to finish
on time. Finally they finished the weaving and
began to cut the marvelous, invisible cloth.

Every hour a court messenger went on horseback to find out how the work progressed.

MESSENGER—How far are you?

FASOLA—We're just cutting the jacket!

MESSENGER—Uhuh! I see, I see.

After a little while, another messenger…

MESSENGER—How is it going?

FASOLA—We're sewing the coat now.

MESSENGER—Already? Look at it! Beautiful!

At last, the day before the procession arrived. The two weavers finished the suit of clothes and rushed it to the emperor's palace.

DOREMI—Here it is, at last, Your Highness! We hope you will be pleased…

EMPEROR—Ahh…let me see my new suit.

FASOLA—Careful, it's very light and delicate.

The coat seemed light indeed. The emperor thought he had nothing in his hands at all, but… of course, he did not admit it.

He held the suit up to the light. But he still didn't see anything...and it seemed to weigh absolutely nothing.

MINISTER—Careful, Your Highness, you dropped the vest. I'll get it.

And the aged minister stooped to pick up the vest, with the help of the dignitary. Neither one saw anything at all; but neither one said as much.

EMPEROR—(Poor me, I'm the only one who can't see these clothes. But I'll never tell.) Thank you. I'll put it on.

WEAVERS—Careful, Emperor. Arrange the train like this...look at yourself in the mirror ...It's a wonderful fit!

The emperor looked in the mirror and
saw himself in drawers and undershirt.
But what could he say?

EMPEROR—Great! I have never looked
so elegant! Get the procession ready at once!
Chamberlain, hold my train.

And the procession went through the city.
No one among the crowds dared to be the
first to say that the emperor was in his underwear,
because no one wanted to appear a fool.
But after a while a child's voice was heard...

CHILD—The emperor isn't wearing any clothes!

CROWD—There speaks the voice of
innocence...The child is right...
The emperor has nothing on!

The emperor glowed with embarrassment, but
it was too late to admit that the clothes
did not exist. So the procession continued,
amidst great laughter, while the chamberlain,
grave and erect, carried the nonexistent
train of the emperor's new coat.

The Three Dogs

Once upon a time there was an old shepherd.
He knew he was dying, and was sad, because
all he had to leave his children were his tiny
cottage and three little lambs. The inheritance
was lowly, but it was all the old man possessed.

FATHER—Children, I must leave you now. Promise
me you will not quarrel, but will divide everything
equally and fairly. Farewell now, my children.

And so saying, the old man closed his eyes and drew
his last breath.

BRENDON—Poor father. Well, little sister, now we are alone in the world. We have only a cottage and three little lambs. Take your choice.

SISTER—If it's all right with you, Brendon, I'd like the cottage.

BRENDON — Certainly, you're a girl and you need a place
to live. I'll take the lambs and go out to seek my fortune.

SISTER — Promise me, Brendon, that if you are not successful,
you will come back home. You know this cottage is
ours to share.

BRENDON — And if I *am* successful, we shall divide my fortune.

Brendon hugged his sister good-by, called his lambs, and set out to seek his fortune. You must realize that a fortune does not necessarily lie around the corner. You must know *how* to find it and you must be very, very patient.

One day Brendon sat under a tree to plan what he

should do next. An old man
with three big dogs came
walking by. He stopped...

OLD MAN

Good day, son.
Would you like to make
a trade? My three dogs
for your three sheep?

BRENDON

Well, I don't know...

OLD MAN

Consider it, my boy.

BRENDON

But my lambs give me wool
to sell for food.

OLD MAN

Use your head, young fellow.
These dogs are very bright,
and each of them has a
special talent. The first
is named "Fetch-me-food."
The second is called
"Eat-em-up." The third is
"Shatter-iron."

BRENDON

Those are silly names, sir,
if you don't mind my saying so.
Anyway, I don't see why you
would want my lambs. Besides,
they have been so good to me.

Brendon and the old man argued for a few minutes, and Brendon decided finally to make the trade. The old man seemed honest, and the three dogs looked friendly. But Brendon could tell that the dogs were not thoroughbreds.

BRENDON—Before you go, sir, I would like to see these dogs in action. If they don't have magic powers, as you claim, then I want my lambs back.

OLD MAN—All right, I'll prove it to you. If you are hungry, call the first dog and see what happens.

BRENDON—"Fetch-me-food," come here.
Hey! Where is he going?
Goodness, he's back already!

OLD MAN—Yes, and look what a good
dinner he brought you. Are you pleased?

BRENDON—Well, yes. But if these dogs
are magic, why do you want to trade?

OLD MAN—Unfortunately, these dogs have
one drawback. The three of them never
want to go in the same direction at the
same time. They pull so hard at their
leashes, that my old arms can no longer

hold them. But you are young and strong and I am sure you can manage them very easily. Good luck to you!

BRENDON—Farewell, and thank you!

So Brendon was left alone, trying to control his dogs. Very soon a carriage passed. Its windows were draped in black as if it were going to a funeral.

Inside the carriage a child was weeping as if
her heart would break. Brendon approached
the carriage curiously and pulled back the
black curtain that draped the window.
Inside he saw a lovely young girl who was
weeping desperately.
Brendon turned to the coachman.

BRENDON—Why is she crying so?

COACHMAN—My dear boy, haven't you heard
about the ferocious dragon that lives nearby?
Every year we must sacrifice a beautiful young
girl to him so he will not attack the village.
This poor girl's name was drawn, and she must be
sacrificed. Unfortunately, she is the king's
daughter, and it is my job as the king's coachman
to take her to the edge of the dragon's den.

BRENDON—Poor girl. I shall follow the carriage.
I cannot believe that no one has the courage
to defend this child.

So Brendon followed the princess. When they arrived at the foot of the mountain, she climbed down from her carriage and walked toward the cave where the dragon lived. The dragon approached the princess— his long, sharp claws and brightly colored wings ready for battle. He licked his chops in anticipation of tasting not only the young princess, but also her satin gown. But...all of a sudden, Brendon sprang up as if out of nowhere, and shouted,

BRENDON—Go to it, "Eat-em-up!" Show us how brave you are, *eat him up!*

So "Eat-em-up" threw himself in front of the dragon and devoured him with one mouthful. Well, actually, it took him a bit more than *one* mouthful. But in five minutes, there was nothing left of the dragon but his teeth and his toenails.

BRENDON—Bravo, "Eat-em-up!" What a wonderful dog you are!

The spectacle of the hound attacking the dragon horrified the princess. But upon realizing the dog had saved her life, she made a deep bow to "Eat-em-up" and smiled sweetly at Brendon.

PRINCESS—My savior! Thank you kind sir. My father will surely reward you for your bravery. Please come with me to my palace.

BRENDON—Your smile is my reward. Farewell, Princess. I must journey on.

PRINCESS—Please, don't leave so quickly. Tell me we shall see each other again.

BRENDON—Very well, My Princess. I shall return in three years.

PRINCESS—Three years! Why so long?

BRENDON—Because I want to see the world, and because I am the son of a poor shepherd and you are the daughter of a king. But I hope that in three years I shall have found my fortune, and then I shall return to ask your hand in marriage. As a pauper, I cannot greet the king.

As soon as Brendon was out of sight, the coachman said,

COACHMAN—Princess,
I could not help overhearing
that your young savior
refused your most gracious
offer to reward him.
So…why don't we tell the king
that *I* was the one who
saved you from the dragon?

PRINCESS—Never!
I shall not tell
such a lie!

COACHMAN—Well, you had
better decide quickly,
or else I shall kill you.
I can very easily go
back to the palace
alone and say that the
dragon had eaten you.
If you want to live,
you'll tell the king
that *I* saved your life!

Tearfully, the princess agreed to lie to her father. She told him that the coachman deserved all the credit for killing the dragon. The king was delighted and praised the coachman very highly.

KING—Noble coachman, for this act of unsurpassed bravery, I shall give you my daughter's hand in marriage. She is still very young, but in two years she will be old enough to marry you.

The princess was glad to have two years before she had to marry the wicked coachman. But, before she knew it, the two years had passed. She wept bitterly at the thought of this dreadful marriage.

KING—What is wrong, little one?

PRINCESS—Father, I am still too young to be married. Couldn't I wait just one more year?

In reality, the princess was still waiting for her real savior, Brendon, to return. But the third year passed even more quickly, and soon the day of the wedding was at hand.

The poor girl didn't have the courage to ask her
father to postpone the wedding any longer,
so she began to prepare herself for the
festivities. I cannot tell you how unhappy
she was! Both her mother and father tried in
vain to comfort her. They could not understand
why she should be so upset on her wedding day.

KING—My child, most girls cry for joy on their
wedding day. But you seem to be
crying from despair.

Meanwhile, that same day, Brendon was
making his way into the city. He had not found
his fortune as he had hoped, because he spent
all his time thinking about the beautiful, young
princess, whom he loved, and was very
anxious to see her again.

As he walked through the city toward the royal palace, he saw preparations for a celebration. The streets were filled with people dressed in their finest clothes. Curious, Brendon stopped a stranger on the street...

BRENDON—Excuse me, kind sir, but why is the city celebrating?

STRANGER—Don't you know? Today, at last, the princess will marry the man who saved her from the vicious dragon three years ago.

BRENDON—But that's a lie! The man who claims he saved her is lying!

SOLDIER—Hey, stranger, don't insult the future prince!

BRENDON—But he has no right to say that! Whoever he is, he's lying!

SOLDIER—Silence! We shall see what the Captain of the Guard has to say about this. You'll learn not to insult royalty!

So, Brendon was imprisoned for speaking out against the future prince. He was put in a dark, empty cell, with a heavy iron chain around his ankle. He was feeling very much alone in the world, without even his dogs. Then he heard a scratching at his cell window...

BRENDON—Whoever that is, go away! If I can't see the princess, I don't want to see anyone. Oh, it's you, "Fetch-me-food," "Eat-em-up," and "Shatter-iron!" I wish you were in here with me. Oh, my good friends! I went out to seek my fortune and ended up in a prison cell. But you are still here, aren't you? Well fellas...

I didn't find my fortune,
At least, not in gold.
I found instead three loyal friends
Who'll be faithful when I'm old.

I guess that's more important,
In fact, it's wealth indeed!
And if we never find that gold,
We still have all we need.

Come in here, dear friends and I shall
pet each of you for the last time.
You come first, "Shatter-iron."
Come here. Hey!
What are you doing?
You've cut through the chains on my
ankles with your teeth!

44

Of course! You are "Shatter-iron" and
that's exactly what you do.
I had forgotten your magic talent.
Quick, my friends, let's get out of this
horrible prison. Maybe there's still
time to stop the princess' wedding.

Brendon jumped on "Eat-em-up's" back and
the four of them ran out of the prison and
into the street. Brendon was very hungry,
so he called "Fetch-me-food" to bring
him something to eat. And can you guess
where "Fetch-me-food" went to find food?

45

He went to the royal palace where everyone was eating the wedding breakfast. Then he went right up to the princess and licked her hand. The princess, of course, recognized the dog immediately.

PRINCESS—Why, it's "Fetch-me-food!"

KING—What on earth are you talking about, my daughter?

QUEEN—Perhaps she's just a bit nervous about the wedding.

PRINCESS—Hurry, father, have that dog followed! Quickly! Have his master brought back to the palace!

KING—All right, all right. Guard, follow the dog! You, young lady, had better have an explanation for this behavior.

The princess beamed. Her eyes filled with joy as she began to tell the true story of how the coachman made her lie to save her life.

KING—So that's how it happened. Guard, take this dishonest coachman away and show him what it's like to live in prison. Soldier, sound the trumpets! Let's give this brave and humble boy who killed the dragon a proper welcome. He and his dogs shall be rewarded at last!

When Brendon arrived at the palace, the king embraced him.

46

The princess stood by and kept repeating,

PRINCESS—At long last you've returned, Brendon, you've returned....

So Brendon and his lovely princess were married that day, and their happiness filled the city with joy. Brendon remembered the promise he had made to his sister, and sent for her to join them in the palace. They say she married one of the dukes, and they too are

very happy. And the three dogs?
Well, they are living in luxury
at the palace, with more bones
than even "Eat-em-up" could ever eat.